Don't Touch My Room

With love for my family…Uvie, Lee, Aaron, and Benjamin

And with enormous thanks to friends…Margaret "Bunny" Gabel,
Alison Cragin Herzig, Jane Lawrence Mali, Sarah Pippin,
and Christina Ward, who asked twice.

P.L.

For Brewster Brockmann,
who sang this song:
"Oh Pipo, Pipo,
I like your brother,
You have such a nice brother,
Oh I like me
I like me."
and for his brother, Pipo, whom
he sang it to.

P.B.

Don't Touch My Room

by

Patricia Lakin

Illustrated by Patience Brewster

Little, Brown and Company

BOSTON   TORONTO

Second Printing

Library of Congress Cataloging in Publication Data

Lakin, Pat.
  Don't touch my room.

  Summary: "Don't touch my room!" becomes "Don't touch my baby!" when a child's antipathy turns into protective feelings towards his new baby brother.
  1. Children's stories, American. [1. Babies — Fiction. 2. Brothers — Fiction] I. Brewster, Patience, ill. II. Title.
PZ7.L1586Do 1985   [E]   84-10063
ISBN 0-316-51230-3

DNP

Published simultaneously in Canada
by Little, Brown & Company (Canada) Limited

PRINTED IN JAPAN

Don't Touch My Room

This is my room.
Here are all my trains.

All this is my city.
And here are my buses and my tram.

Here's my closet. I go inside. Then I close the doors
and pretend it's an elevator.

This is where I keep my books.
I know where *everything* is.

They want to change my room around.
They'll give me a carpet. Buses can't go on a carpet!
And they'll take away this wall. I *love* this wall!

They say everything will be bigger and better.
I say everything will be worse.

But they say I'll need a bigger room to share
    when we get my baby brother.
I don't want to share anything.
I don't want a baby brother, either.

What if he cries all night?
It will give me terrible dreams.

What if the baby grabs all my toys and knocks down my city?
How can I play?

Why don't we just forget about it.
We don't need a baby at all.
Then we won't have to change anything.
But they say we're getting him anyway.

Maybe he could live somewhere else. We could visit.
They say that way they couldn't get to know the baby.

They say wait and see.

My new room will be terrific.

My new baby brother will be loads of fun.

I'm not so sure.

But just in case...

I'm moving.

This can be my room.

And here is where I'll put my sign.
It will say, in giant letters,
DON'T TOUCH MY ROOM.

Don't Touch My Things

They touched everything.
"It's for your new room," they said.
"It's for the new baby," I said.

First they packed all my buses and cars and trains
   and my tram and my books.
They took down my city.
Then they moved out my bed and my lamp and my night table
   and my favorite pillow.

All the toys got put into boxes and put away in the cellar.

All my clothes and bed stuff went into the living room, where I'll sleep.

The wall…broken to bits and carried away.

And now my room…gone. Everything's gone.

My closet doors that I used for a pretend elevator are off and gone, too.

Everything's terrible.

At night, in the living room, where my bed is,
   the streetlight shines.

Even through my closed eyes.

When I look out the window there,
   I get scared by the branches of the big tree.

I can't sleep.

I can't play, either.

"Don't touch the tools.
   Not safe," the workers say.

So, I have to do lots of secret stuff.

When it's nighttime, I creep back to the space where
my old room used to be.
I turn on the work light and play.

I grab a wrench. I'm a pirate.

14

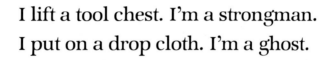

I lift a tool chest. I'm a strongman.
I put on a drop cloth. I'm a ghost.

Sometimes, I just walk around and think how *I'd* make my
new room. Trapdoor here. Tree house there. Swimming pool
over there.

But they find out about almost everything.

"Stay out of the work area. Too dangerous, night or day," they say.
And at night they cover the living room window with a cloth.
No light gets through.
"Now you can sleep," they say. "And no peeking in your new room.
Not until it's ready."

"Come and see," they finally say.
I'm scared to look.

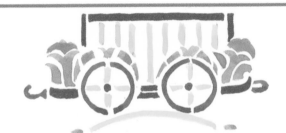

My wall! Just like the old one. It's terrific!

My closet door. It doesn't close like an elevator. It's terrible.

I look inside. My toys.

There are my cars, my buses, my tram and trains, and my books. All back. Great!

And the carpet. It is flat. Buses can go on it.

"I can put my city here," I say.

"What's all this stuff?"

"For the baby," they say.

"No fair. He's taking up all my new room. What about me?"

"Well, there is a surprise," they say.

"What is it?"

"Find it," they say.

I look everywhere. I can't find it.

So they take me over to the new wall.

"Push," they say.

I push. Whaam! A secret door opens.

It's big enough only for me.

I crawl inside.

"Where did you get this little room?" I say.

They just smile.

"I'll put my city inside," I say.

A secret door to a secret city. Not for babies.

Not for grown-ups. Just for me!

And here is where I'll put my sign.

It will say, in giant letters,

DON'T TOUCH MY THINGS.

FOR MOM
AND DADDY
3

22

Don't Touch My Baby

The baby came. A boy. Just like I said.
They called him Benjamin.
I called him *Awful.*

At first, all he did was sleep, eat, and spit up.
All they did was spend every second with *him.*
"Not now," they said. They were feeding the baby.
Or diapering him. Or burping him. Or cleaning
   his spit up. Or putting him to sleep.

23

"Now, what would *you* like to play?" they said.
"Nothing," I said.

24

So, I'd go to my room and push on the
special spot on the wall.
Alacazam! My secret door opened to my secret
place. That's where I keep my city.

Then he got older.
They started calling him Benji.
I started calling him *Worse*.

He tried to pull my hair,
   or scratch my face,
   or pinch my nose.
"Don't!" I yelled.
He just laughed.

So then I'd have to hug him really hard.
Sometimes he cried.
"Don't touch the baby," they said.

27

But I cried, too.

When he grabbed my car, or sucked on
    my bicycle handle, or knocked down my castle,
    or ripped up my books, or spit up on my bed.
"Make him say he's sorry," I said.
"There. There. He's only a baby," they said.

28

Benji got bigger.

They started calling him Benji — *Watch Out!*

I started calling him Benji *the Pest*.

That's because he always crawled around after me.

So we'd have to play dog.

And he'd always laugh when I tossed him the red ball.

So I'd have to do it about a million times.

Now Benji's even bigger.
They still call him Benji.
But sometimes they call him *Bad Boy.*
"He's only a baby," I say.
That's what I said when Benji tried to stand.

The table was set.

Milk, lamb chops, mashed potatoes, carrots, peas,
  plates, knives, forks, spoons, one vase with flowers,
  and the candles all fell to the floor.

They screamed at him.

I had no choice.

"C'mon, Benji," I said.

We crawled to my secret door, opened it,
and went inside to play with my secret
city. Before I closed the door
I told them, "DON'T TOUCH MY BABY!"